Amelie and Nanette

Snowflakes and Fairy Wishes

"Sharing Christmas with your best friend is the best present EVER!"

by Sophie Tilley

BLOOMSBURY

LONDON NEW DELHI NEW YORK SYDNEY

Amelie and Nanette are best friends
and have been FOREVER.

Because there is nothing nicer than having a best friend
to share your secrets and adventures with . . .

Amelie

Nanette

It was December and snowflakes had begun to fall.
Christmas was just days away.

Amelie and Nanette were bubbling over with excitement
preparing for Christmas and also, very importantly,
preparing for the school Christmas party.

Nanette was at Amelie's house and there was LOTS to do . . .

paper chains to make,

Christmas cards to write, presents to wrap . . .

and yummy scrummy snowflake fairy cakes to bake.

The fun part was doing it all with your best friend.

Together, Amelie and Nanette gathered decorations for the Christmas tree . . .

sparkly stars,

a friendly fairy,

colourful baubles,

stripy candy canes.

Then (with a little help from Pilou the dog) they set about decorating it.
And, as they did, they sang magical Christmas tunes.

The girls were so busy that they hadn't noticed how much snow had fallen outside.
"Oh, look!" squeaked Nanette. "Heaps and heaps of LOVELY snow!"
"Ooooh!" said Amelie. "Let's make a snowman!"

Nanette was SO excited that she ran outside without her hat and coat!

"It's the biggest snowman ever!" said Nanette,
wrapping her scarf around his neck.

Amelie put her hat on his head.
"He's the biggest, nicest, warmest snowman now," she giggled.

As the snowflakes continued to float and flutter to the ground,
the two friends had the most wonderfully silly snow-time fun . . .

jumping and rolling around . . .

throwing snowballs . . .

sledging . . .

. . . and filling the garden with beautiful snow angels.

Soon, though, they were feeling just a little bit chilly.
"Let's go inside and make our costumes for the party," said Amelie.
"Good idea," said Nanette, shivering. "I'm freezing!"

Inside, they cuddled up under a cosy duvet with a warming
mug of hot chocolate while their wet clothes dried in front of the fire.
Nanette had a very red nose and rosy cheeks.

"ACHOO!" she sneezed.

"You look like Rudolf the red-nosed reindeer!" said Amelie and they both giggled loudly.

The school party was fancy dress and
the friends were going to be fairies.
They stuck silver stars onto cut-out wings,
twizzled tinselly bits into hairbands and
sprinkled glittery sparkles onto magic wands.

But then, Nanette did another big sneeze - "ACHOO!"
"I'm feeling a bit funny," she said.
"I think I want to go home."

She didn't even finish her costume.

When the day of the Christmas party arrived,
Amelie waited excitedly at the school gate for Nanette . . .
but Nanette didn't come!
It turned out that she had a very bad cold and had to stay in bed.

Amelie was sad. How could the party EVER
be the same without her best friend there?

Poor Nanette was sad too! She was feeling poorly,
missing her friend AND missing the party!

Luckily, after a few days, Nanette started to feel much better
and she was allowed a VERY SPECIAL VISITOR . . .

and the very special visitor had a very special surprise . . .

Nanette couldn't believe her eyes. Amelie was dressed in her fairy outfit looking lovely and sparkly, and she'd brought along Pilou too, who was wearing reindeer antlers and a red coat.

Nanette clapped her hands with glee.
"Thank you so much. You've really cheered me up!"

But there was an even better surprise to come.
Amelie had finished Nanette's fairy costume!

The girls danced around excitedly in their home-made fairy dresses,
waving their sparkly wands and making festive fairy wishes.

Amelie gave her friend a big hug.
"I'm so glad you're better, I missed you SO much!" said Amelie.
"I missed you, too!" replied Nanette. "Thank you for my fairy costume!"

"Well, you ARE my best friend!" said Amelie.
"And there are more surprises for you in my magic Christmas bag."

There were cards and little presents from all Nanette's school friends, and sparkly crackers,
and Amelie and her mummy had baked special Christmas fairy cakes for them to share.
As they tucked into the delicious cakes, they chatted all about
the magic of Christmas day to come . . .

"Thank you for making Christmas so special!" smiled Nanette.
And they both agreed that sharing Christmas with
your best friend is the best present EVER!

For Drew, my 'Mr Noel' x

Bloomsbury Publishing, London, New Delhi, New York and Sydney

First published in Great Britain in 2014 by Bloomsbury Publishing Plc
50 Bedford Square, London, WC1B 3DP

This paperback edition first published in 2015
Text and illustrations copyright © Sophie Tilley 2014
The moral right of the author/ illustrator has been asserted

A CIP catalogue record for this book is available from the British Library

ISBN 978 1 4088 3664 4 (HB)   ISBN 978 1 4088 3665 1 (PB)   ISBN 978 1 4088 3862 4 (eBook)

1 3 5 7 9 10 8 6 4 2

Printed in China by Leo Paper Products, Heshan, Guangdong
www.bloomsbury.com

BLOOMSBURY is a registered trademark of Bloomsbury Publishing Plc

All papers used by Bloomsbury Publishing are natural, recyclable products
made from wood grown in well-managed forests.
The manufacturing processes conform to the environmental regulations of the country of origin